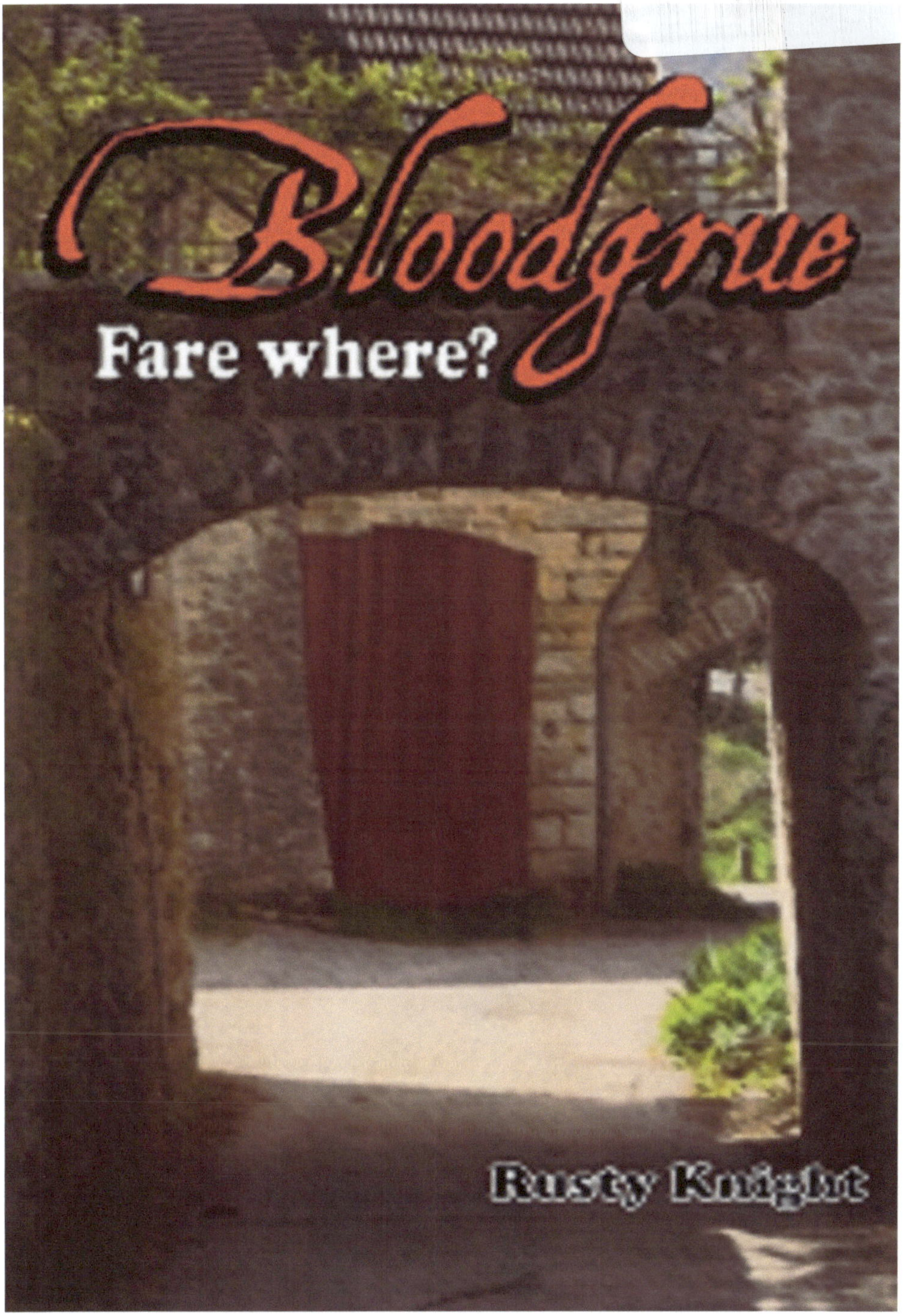

Bloodgrue

Fare where?

Rusty Knight

Bloodgrue
Volume 3: Business

Welcome to our serial stories!

If you're not familiar with our serial series, think of them as a favorite nighttime program that continues with a new episode each week, only it is in a book format. These are stories that don't necessarily have an end planned for them, or if they do, it's a long way off unlike many television series that we get interested in, only to have them go off air.

Serial stories are a great way to keep you entertained and on edge waiting to see what will happen next, in short enough episodes to enjoy on a lunch break, or before going to bed. Although our stories are designed to be read one episode per week, unlike TV stories, if you just can't wait for the next episode, you can get another one any time.

Be sure to download!

It is a good idea to download the book when you first purchase it. Then, just read them at your leisure.

Please feel free to let us know what you think of our serial stories. It's a new trend and may take some getting used to, but we've had positive feedback in the past with them.

Now, it's time to enjoy!

InUPress

We would like to acknowledge the following for their work in the production of this series.

Cover design, C S Burgar
Editing, Donna Shumaker (Aria)

As producer at InUPress.ca and author of the Bloodgrue serial short-story series, I thank you for reading the Bloodgrue book.

Yours, Rusty Knight.

To be continued with *Bloodgrue Volume 4: Attractions*
It will be found at *InUPress.ca* **and Amazon**
Previous books in the series now available at *www.inupress.ca* **and Amazon:**
- *Bloodgrue Volume 1: Fare Where!*
- *Bloodgrue Volume 2: Breaths*

Bloodgrue
Volume 3: Business

Previously on *Bloodgrue* **Winter 27 Lizard**: *Bloodgrue traveled into Western Madison to find his friend, the peasant-hero Noah, had purchased Red Square. They formed an impromptu court to hold a trial for the son of a ward councilman, who stood accused of bullying a family. He also stood accused of stealing all their food and coins. In the trial the boy was found guilty of all charges and he lost his left hand. The court paid a small amount of restitution to the impoverished family, thus was set the First Justice Court of Western Madison.*

Bloodgrue
By *Rusty Knight*

Episode eleven, 'Teptun Square & Market's Blue Hair'

Bloodgrue
Volume 3: Business

We continue on …

Spring 1 Raccoon, Bloodgrue has just arrived in Low Docks ward in the heavy rain. The gods deemed it hilarious to drop heavy rains on Bloodgrue along with stiff east cold breaths. He left 4212 Willow Road to look for work early; before gods-rise. The world is attempting to hold onto the last visages of winter.

Standing on Water Way Street, Bloodgrue looks out at Dock A. Hating water at the best of times; Bloodgrue ponders the irony of his working the North Docks, and having a mild phobia of open water. Gods are funny sometimes, sometimes!

The new clothes gifted from Onar fit well and help attract customers, as much as the Western Madison clothes do that Guilda made him. Today, its Onar's clothes that Bloodgrue wears. Bolstering his resolve, Bloodgrue walks towards a group of three who are walking towards dry ground. Huh! Dry ground! In these rains that doesn't exist, so let's say, solid ground.

The three step up onto the paving stones before Bloodgrue has to step down onto the dock planks.

Smiling, Bloodgrue tries addressing them in jal speech first. "God's-grace and good fate gentle folk. May I be of aid?"

While saying this, Bloodgrue is jostled by a dock worker headed out onto the docks. Bloodgrue's hand reflexively checks his new coin pouch while he smiles.

It's time for evening meal and the outters look hungry and tired. The century-old toyfem answers in course jal. "Yes. We need a dragoman. I am looking for an old friend I wish to visit. I have been away for some time … oh my … my rudeness, god's grace and good fate young man. Do you know where I can find a dragoman?"

Bloodgrue smiles hugely and answers in a positive manner. "I am Apprentice Dragoman Bloodgrue. I know North Docks very well. Who are you looking for? I may know them."

The crone smiles a toothless grin as she waits a moment, then she replies. "Sure, she used to go by the name Blue Hair. Do you know her?"

Bloodgrue nods. "Yes, yes I do, her stall is in Teptun Square and Market. It will be dark before we arrive there, so she will have left. We should find an Inn here for the night. My fee is food and lodging and four dusters to get you to Blue Hair."

The crone looks around, then nods, "Yes, I need a rest and some food anyway. What Inn do you recommend?"

Bloodgrue ponders her gear then he answers. "I recommend the Drop Bucket. It has low rates, but decent fare. Four Dyns will set us all up for the night, with cold meals."

Bloodgrue
Volume 3: Business

The woman smiles, satisfied. "Yes, I like that. My name is Ladya. Lead the way, Bloodgrue."

Bloodgrue takes the group to 137 Water Way and into the Drop Bucket Inn for the night.

Spring 2 Raccoon, Ladya is eager to start out, well before gods-rise, and Bloodgrue is ready to accommodate. Walking the more than five kilometers to Teptun, Bloodgrue is talking up a storm with the three clients. But, Bloodgrue is not getting much personal information from them.

Entering Teptun Square & Market through the north, from the Elmar Road entrance, Bloodgrue leads to the fountain, finding that Blue Hair never came in today. Bloodgrue addresses the trio. "Well, we can wait for her to show tomorrow if you like?"

Ladya smiles, "Yes, find us an inn for today, Bloodgrue."

Bloodgrue take the trio to the Tempest Inn and Tavern, setting them up for the night.

Spring 3 Raccoon, Bloodgrue stretches, having slept poorly, as he is not feeling right about something. He walks down to the tavern to find Ladya and her companions, Menya and Turos, waiting to travel already, a full hour before gods-rise.

Menya is a jalfem and she walks the sea-walk which seems out of place on land. She is wearing well used leather armour and an old short-sword. Her friend, Turos, has a well used short-sword as well, and also walks the sea-walk. Both are in their fifties and all day yesterday they didn't sit right in Bloodgrue's mind. But their eagerness today is setting off even more alarms.

Blue Hair told Bloodgrue some things about her past, and this is coming to Bloodgrue now as a bad thing today. But what, or why he doesn't know.

"Okay, let's go Bloodgrue. Show us where Blue Hair keeps her stall." Instructs Ladya eagerly.

Bloodgrue checks his concealed dagger's hilt to be sure it's handy.

Noah and Bloodgrue had worked for three hours on his skills with it last time Bloodgrue was with Noah. It may not be much, but he may need it today.

"Okay, let's go. Blue Hair is usually there around gods-rise." answers Bloodgrue solemnly.

He remembers someone telling him about the feats Blue Hair can perform with her scimitar. The scimitar she wears everywhere she goes. They say she trains Weapon Masters. But Bloodgrue has never seen Blue Hair draw the weapon from its scabbard.

The walk is pleasant, as it is warm, with the gods breathing moderately strong east. The broken cover in the sphere promises some shade from the heat of the gods.

Bloodgrue
Volume 3: Business

Arriving in the square, half-an-hour after gods-rise, Bloodgrue leads the group directly over to the central fountain and stall 74.

Not wanting to tip off Ladya and company, that Bloodgrue can call on nearby help if need be, Bloodgrue refrains from signalling anyone. He stands near Blue Hair to start introductions, but Blue Hair stops him.

"Ladya, are you here in peace, or for trouble?" asks Blue Hair earnestly.

Ladya steps in close and menacingly. Looking into Blue Hair's face, she grinds out through gritting gums. "You … owe me, thirty years … three-hundred Flairs and my career."

Blue Hair leans boldly forward and sternly replies. "You got caught stealing. The courts found you guilty … You ran. I caught you again and took you in … That doubled your sentence. You lost everything because you broke the law and then tried to flee justice. Getting caught both times cost you … I owe you nothing. Step away."

Ladya straightens and looking at the two she brought with her, she commands them. "Do what I paid you for! Slay her and extract the debt she owes me!"

Turos looks at Menya and shakes his head. Menya looks at Ladya giving her both of their answers. "From what she just said, she owes you nothing. You haven't paid us enough to commit murder."

Ladya screams, and then pulls a knife from the left sleeve of her tunic, madly rushing at Blue Hair.

Blue Hair draws her scimitar as she steps back two steps. The scimitar gleams from loving care of a master warrior. The light that strikes the blade reflects off completely.

Before Ladya has closed in with her rusted knife, Blue Hair has unlimbered her scimitar and had a few swirls of motion.

Bloodgrue draws his dagger and steps up to the two mercenary sailors. Pointing to the battle he shakes his head.

Both mercenaries move their hands away from their weapons, indicating their desire not to be involved.

Being naturally quicker, Ladya gets inside Blue Hair's defense, attacking the merchant.

But with Blue Hair's skill, she deflects the attack before it does serious damage.

The knife drags across Blue Hair's tunic.

Bloodgrue
Volume 3: Business

Blue Hair's first swing comes across Ladya's right leg and continues across her left leg, quickly dropping Ladya to the square's warm paving stones. But proving her reputation of no mercy, Blue Hair brings the scimitar around in a blur, across Ladya's chest, almost instantly killing Ladya.

Blue Hair stands straight.

Looking at the two mercenaries, Blue Hair growls at them menacingly. "Do you want to avenge her now?"

The two shake their heads negatively.

To Blue Hair's detriment, no City Watch was near at the moment. But in a few minutes, as Blue Hair is cleaning her scimitar on Ladya's legging, a City Watch private approaches.

"Blue Hair, I see a body and you have a weapon in hand. I am afraid you must wait here until Sergeant Maynard arrives. As well, as well along with any witnesses I identify right now."

He looks around him, and then starts pointing, picking out twenty people, including Bloodgrue and the two mercenaries. Then choosing a middle-class servant, he instructs her. "Go to the city watch post at 3017 Osmo Road and inform Sergeant Maynard that Private Penstal is reporting there has been a murder at stall 74 in Teptun's, and be quick. There will be a duster in it for you."

The jalfem takes off quickly northward.

Nearly seven hours pass before Sergeant Maynard rides up on a horse. Along with him are two other City Watch men. He dismounts and walks to the body.

Looking over Ladya, Sergeant Maynard looks impressed.

The private waits for Maynard.

Then the sergeant speaks with Private Penstal.

They come over to the group. "Okay, so you, Blue Hair, killed the outter? Why?"

Blue Hair, having sheathed her scimitar a long while ago, after cleaning and inspecting it; answers the City Watch Sergeant straight forward. "Sergeant Maynard, it was self-defence, as she threatened me and drew her knife, attacking. I defended myself."

Maynard frowns. "A little overkill don't you think? Killing her when all she had was a rusty four-inch knife?"

Bloodgrue
Volume 3: Business

Blue Hair answers quickly but evenly, without emotion. "A weapon is still a weapon. The skill is the matter. You know that."

Maynard turns to the mercenaries. "Do you think the attacker had the skill to harm Blue Hair?"

Both shake their heads and Turos answers. "No, she was old and feeble."

Bloodgrue offers. "To be fair, she came here to kill Blue Hair, and she paid these two to help her kill Blue Hair. It was a matter of self-defence against a possibility of three attackers. I see no wrong done by Blue Hair."

Nine others confirm Bloodgrue's witnessing. No one else can say they saw anything.

Sergeant Maynard addresses Turos and Menya. "Are you two registered mercenaries?"

Both pale and shake their heads no.

"That will be a 5 Dyns fine each. It would have been goal time if you had drawn weapons. I want you out of North Docks until you register. If you leave without paying your fine, may the gods help you if you ever get seen in North Docks again." Instruct Maynard.

Turning to Blue Hair, he frowns even deeper. "You … You know better … But you were vindicated by ten … So you are free to go with a warning and a one Flair fine. I want it paid within a six day. Or you will spend thirty days in the goal … Now I have your mess to clean up."

Blue Hair stops Sergeant Maynard and offers him two Flairs. "One for the fine and one for the City Watch fund … My apology for all the trouble, Sergeant Maynard."

Maynard looks at the two coins, and then nods. "The fine is paid and we thank you … Well done Blue Hair. The warning is removed from your record."

Blue Hair gives the mercenaries each a chicken carcass.

Blue Hair secretively shows Bloodgrue an old coin pouch. Whispering to Bloodgrue she utters. "This fell off her belt while I was cleaning my scimitar. She had eleven dusters and seven Dyns left."

The City Watch removes the corpse and the crowd of witnesses disperse.

Bloodgrue helps Blue Hair clean and close her stall. Then they both leave for their homes, with the incident not mentioned again.

To be continued …

Bloodgrue
Volume 3: Business

In the next episode twelve, '*Lena*',

Bloodgrue will be stunned as he negotiates work with a client. Searching for, but not seeing the woman who stuns him again, Bloodgrue asks Blue Hair for her help finding the young jalfem.

Bloodgrue
Volume 3: Business

Awesome! You finished an episode of '*Bloodgrue*'.

Let us know what you think of it by going to this this link: www.inupress.ca While you are there, you should join the Inevitable Unicorn Press e-mail subscription list to receive news and updates about work from our authors such as; Rusty Knight, Brian Hill and Aria. When you sign up for the e-mail list, you will receive a free pdf. This free pdf changes with time. In February 2016 the gift was a copy of Rusty Knight's biography of the protagonists, the Black Swans, from his novel, '*Laret*'. Later in 2016, the bonus is an issue from the serial series, '*Lanis*'.

While on the home page of InUPress.ca leave a comment telling us what you think of our author's work, or the website. We appreciate your time and we will respond to questions and comments.

Thank you for reading.
Yours,
Rusty Knight of Inevitable Unicorn Press.
www.inupress.ca

Bloodgrue
Volume 3: Business

Welcome to our serial stories!

If you're not familiar with our serial series, think of them as a favorite nighttime program that continues with a new episode each week, only this is in a book format. These are stories that don't necessarily have an end planned for them, or if they do, it's a long way off unlike many television series that we get interested in, only to have them go off air.

Serial stories are a great way to keep you entertained and on edge waiting to see what will happen next, in short enough episodes to enjoy on a lunch break, or before going to bed. Although our stories are designed to be read one episode per week, unlike TV stories, if you just can't wait for the next episode, you can get another one any time.

Be sure to download!

It is a good idea to download episodes when you first purchase them. Then, read them at your leisure.

Please feel free to let us know what you think of our serial stories. It's a new trend and may take some getting used to, but we've had positive feedback in the past with them.

Now, it's time to enjoy!

InUPress

We would like to acknowledge the following for their work in the production of this series.

Cover design, C S Burgar
Editing, Donna Shumaker (Aria)

Bloodgrue
Volume 3: Business

Previously on *Bloodgrue* **Spring 1 Raccoon**: *Bloodgrue was in Low Dock ward and was hired on to take clients to see Blue Hair in Teptun Square and Market. It turned out the client wanted more than to meet Blue Hair. The client ended up dead. The City Watch ended up two Flairs richer and two mercenaries wound up with two chicken carcasses.*

Bloodgrue
By Rusty Knight
Episode twelve, 'Lena'

Bloodgrue
Volume 3: Business

We continue on …

Spring 27 Raccoon, is a day not like any other here in Teptun Square and Market, which is filled with outters as well as locals. Bloodgrue left 4212 before gods-rise to get a jump on clients, having decided it was easier to get clients on a cold partially covered day in Teptun's, so that is where Bloodgrue walked to.

With leaving before gods-rise on a pleasant day, it is afternoon before Bloodgrue arrives in the square. Drumming up business used to be difficult, but recently that has changed. Bloodgrue has new clothing from two sources. One source was his peasant-hero friend Noah, over in Western Madison. Noah fleeced a merchant thug from Velan and with the winnings purchased Bloodgrue a complete set on new clothes. Two; Bloodgrue's new initiatives encouraged his master to take another look into Bloodgrue's future. When Bloodgrue impressed him, Onar gathered new clothes for Bloodgrue, though he did charge Bloodgrue two Royal Flairs for the clothes, even though they are only worth one Flair and five Dyns. Still they are new clothes. Today Bloodgrue is wearing the newer set of clothes from Onar, hoping to reel in a client quickly.

Walking on this cold day, among the crowd of business merchants and tradesmen with their customers, Bloodgrue observers everyone, watching for tells of those lost or searching.

Near one o'clock in the afternoon he is in luck as Bloodgrue is strolling near the central fountain.

A group of three are standing looking around confused. One is a well dressed, upper-middle-class style toymal, asking people questions. The other two stand nearby silently. One of these two is an elfmal who is obviously a labourer and probably the grunt for the group. The other is a half-elfmal hunter with his bow and sword ready for a fight, likely the groups muscle.

Bloodgrue approaches the trio and in his best toy speech he addresses the group's leader. "God's-grace and good fate master, may I be of aid? I am Apprentice Dragoman Bloodgrue."

The toymal looks Bloodgrue over and shrugs. "I doubt it, but maybe. I need a specific, good specimen of a Spertan. But I need it for a Mage's task. Do you think you can qualify yourself to help?"

Bloodgrue beams his smile that is becoming famous in the North Docks. "Of course I can help you. You are in the wrong place master. On two counts; for a good Spertan specimen of any kind, you want to be down on a dock. For mage specimens, you want to be over on Mage's Pyre Rock ward. I can get you there for one Dyns a day, plus lodging and food."

The toymal looks at Bloodgrue suspiciously. "I am Mage Elmar. If you mess with me I will turn you into a toad and then freeze you in a block of ice and let the gods slowly unthaw you in a children's play yard."

Bloodgrue
Volume 3: Business

Bloodgrue grimaces slightly at the thought of possibly unthawing in a block of ice as a toad in a children's play yard. Not a good thing any way you look at it.

"Sounds fair to me, I honor my work. Pay the fee now for the three days to get there. The lodging and food you take care of as we go. At the docks, if we require more time, then you can pay as we go. But I will get you where you need to be Master Elmar. And who are your two friends?"

Elmar huffs then shrugs again. Pointing to the half elf, "That is my hunter Micra; my servant is the elf Lanter. Never pay them much mind, unless I ask you to. When do we start out?"

Bloodgrue starts to answer when a gruff appearing toymal pushes Micra into the fountain and shouts "Get out of Mount Oryn. It aint no place for halfers. You scum don't belong here dirtying our city with your filth."

Elmar takes exception to this and grabs the man's shoulder as Micra draws his longsword in anger.

Bloodgrue, seeing issues arising with a new client, shakily steps in between the folks with his hands held shoulder high. "Hold on here. There are laws about assault. And we can have this farmer locked in the goal for assaulting Micra. No need for weapons."

At that moment Bloodgrue is stunned, not by a blow, but by a sight.

A young woman glances at him as he looks her way. She is a seventeen-years-old, or so, a jalfem more beautiful than any Bloodgrue has ever seen. Not even Luenen is in his mind now.

Bloodgrue smiles and blushes as their eyes meet. He can't look away.

A voice shouts in his ear. "The damn farmer pushed Micra in the fountain and insulted him. I want restitution for damages to my property that Micra is carrying."

Bloodgrue breaks eye contact and looks at the face inches from his. "Ok then, if the farmer won't pay restitution, do to him what you said you would do to me. Simple, right?"

Bloodgrue looks back away, looking for the girl. But she isn't there.

'Damn the seven hells. Now where did she go?' Thinks Bloodgrue as he glances around quickly.

The farmer is reluctantly handing Elmar five Dyns, as Bloodgrue returns his attention to the scene.

Micra is standing next to Bloodgrue with water dripping off of him. Micra tells Bloodgrue. "It happens occasionally. The master roasted the last fellow who assaulted me. We had to run for three days before the lynch mob gave up on chasing us. Thanks for calming him."

Bloodgrue shrugs; still disappointed he couldn't see *her* again.

Bloodgrue
Volume 3: Business

The assault ordeal dealt with, and Bloodgrue's coin pouch three Dyns heavier, he turns to Elmar. "Time to start walking, we will spend some time on the streets. It's over twenty-eight kilometres to Mage's Pyre Rock."

Spring 29 Raccoon, the heat and fierce breaths of the gods are tormenting everyone and everything. Not one barge is out on the open water as the gods breathe so fiercely.

The group arrived on Mangrove Avenue a couple minutes ago, in mid-afternoon.

Bloodgrue knows who he is looking for; the man is a net fisherman by the name of Jessen. Jessen hangs around Dock A when not out on the river, or in a tavern, or at home. Looking earnestly among the crowd, Bloodgrue eventually finds the tall toymal. "God's-grace and good fate Jessen, how goes your day in this gods breath?"

The fisherman smiles eagerly. "Are you buying today Blood, or bringing me customers?"

Bloodgrue gestures to Elmar. "Customer, my friend, this is Mage Elmar and company. They have a request of you. Shall I leave you to business a minute? I will stay in case Master Elmar needs more assistance."

The two men haggle for half-an-hour. Then a happy Elmar approaches Bloodgrue and hands him a Flair. "Dragoman, you brought me to the right place. Jessen had what I need and at below what I was expecting to pay. So here is a tip. What is your address so I may call on you in the future?"

Bloodgrue puts the coin in his pouch as he answers diligently. "My residence is 4212 Willow Road, Master Elmar. Call on me any time. God's-grace and good fate Master. Unless there is more, I will be on my way. I have another engagement to tend to soon."

Elmar clasps arm with Bloodgrue. "No, young dragoman, we have completed our business. God's-grace and good fate, thank you so much."

Parting ways, Bloodgrue sets out immediately, heading for Teptun Square and Market, fighting the gods weather to do so. Bloodgrue sweats out as much water as he drinks today.

Spring 31 Raccoon, Bloodgrue walks into Teptun Square and Market from the east side, sweating more than a race horse after a two mile run. The continued heat is draining Bloodgrue, but at least the gods stop breathing so hard on Quantos. Plus, they decided to provide partial cover today to tease mortals occasionally with cooling shade.

Looking over the market, Bloodgrue can see that even now in the middle of the day, the crowds are half their usual size.

Bloodgrue
Volume 3: Business

Bloodgrue walks south-west to the centre of the square, watching as he walks, looking for the person he wants to meet. He walks the alleys between the stalls, first east to west, then north to south, going back and forth, watch and looking. It's not a customer he is looking for today; he is looking for a specific person.

Finally, nearly two and a half hours later, Bloodgrue is exhausted. He walks to the fountain and washes off.

An idea strikes him. Bloodgrue walks to stall 74 and he sees Blue Hair has two carcasses left with a customer. The jalfem customer buys one carcass and talks with Blue Hair for twenty minutes.

When she leaves, Bloodgrue approaches the stall.

"Blue Hair, I am buying your chicken for one Flair."

Blue Hair looks Bloodgrue over, and then asks. "So the heat has gotten to you? Do you have a Flair? You know there are no refunds."

Bloodgrue takes the gold coin from his pouch, hesitating a moment as he thinks about this … then he hands it to Blue Hair. "I know the protocol."

Blue Hair takes the coin and tosses it into her coin box with the other Flairs, Dyns and dusters. She takes the chicken off the hook. Handing it to Bloodgrue she asks. "What is it my friend?"

Bloodgrue looks the chicken over after accepting it. Not one pin feather, not one imperfection in the whole carcass. He smiles as he looks up, knowing Onar won't appreciate the Flair cost of this chicken.

Bloodgrue says to Blue Hair. "I am wondering if you know a person I am looking for? She is a jalfem of about sixteen-years-old, or so. I have never seen her here before. I saw her a few days ago and I am wondering if you know her?"

Blue Hair laughs heartily. "So the bug finally caught you apprentice. Describe this young fem for me."

Bloodgrue stops, realizing even though she is beautiful, he can describe her grey eyes, black hair and such. The description describes almost every jalfem.

Bloodgrue stumbles over his words saying, "I think I just bought a one Flair chicken for supper."

He chuckles embarrassed. "She has grey eyes and long black hair … wait I recall now she was tall; I would say about five-feet ten-inches, maybe one-hundred and sixty to one-hundred and seventy pounds, around sixteen or seventeen-years-old. No unusual markings or jewelry. But that is all I recall, I got lost in her eyes … Damn, Blue Hair, is that how this love thing happens?'

Bloodgrue
Volume 3: Business

Blue Hair pats Bloodgrue's shoulder. "I call it infatuation, love is long term and you have to know the person. But the Shes have over one thousand forms of love … even for all their hatred and anger. I know a few young women matching that description, apprentice. I know a few ugly ones too. But I will point out the beauties over time when we are together. You tell me if she is the right one. When we find her, I will introduce you two. Deal?"

Bloodgrue hugs Blue Hair without warning, almost getting punched for his effort, but then getting hugged in return.

After settling back and regaining control, Bloodgrue looks around.

Blue Hair offers Bloodgrue. "Since you are here and you have about an hour before you have to leave, to go feed Onar, let's work on your script."

To be continued …

In the next episode thirteen, 'Lost',

Bloodgrue escorts home a lost teenager. On his way back home a rogue beggar stops Bloodgrue asking for more than a few coins. The beggar claims to be one of Pandora's, but Bloodgrue suspects otherwise.

Bloodgrue
Volume 3: Business

Awesome! You finished an episode of '*Bloodgrue*'.

Let us know what you think of it by going to this this link: www.inupress.ca While you are there, you should join the Inevitable Unicorn Press e-mail subscription list to receive news and updates about work from our authors such as; Rusty Knight, Brian Hill and Aria. When you sign up for the e-mail list, you will receive a free pdf. This free pdf changes with time. In February 2016 the gift was a copy of Rusty Knight's biography of the protagonists, the Black Swans, from his novel, '*Laret*'. Later in 2016, the bonus is an issue from the serial series, '*Lanis*'.

While on the home page of InUPress.ca leave a comment telling us what you think of our author's work, or the website. We appreciate your time and we will respond to questions and comments.

Thank you for reading.
Yours,
Rusty Knight of Inevitable Unicorn Press.
www.inupress.ca

Bloodgrue
Volume 3: Business

Welcome to our serial stories!

If you're not familiar with our serial series, think of them as a favorite nighttime program that continues with a new episode each week, only this is in a book format. These are stories that don't necessarily have an end planned for them, or if they do, it's a long way off unlike many television series that we get interested in, only to have them go off air.

Serial stories are a great way to keep you entertained and on edge waiting to see what will happen next, in short enough episodes to enjoy on a lunch break, or before going to bed. Although our stories are designed to be read one episode per week, unlike TV stories, if you just can't wait for the next episode, you can get another one any time.

Be sure to download!

It is a good idea to download episodes when you first purchase them. Then, just read them at your leisure.

Please feel free to let us know what you think of our serial stories. It's a new trend and may take some getting used to, but we've had positive feedback in the past with them.

Now, it's time to enjoy!

InUPress

We would like to acknowledge the following for their work in the production of this series.

Cover design, C S Burgar
Editing, Donna Shumaker (Aria)

Bloodgrue
Volume 3: Business

Previously on *Bloodgrue* **Spring 27 Raccoon**: *Bloodgrue was in Teptun Square, negotiating with a client, when he was stunned. Recovering somewhat, he continued to take his client to Mage's Pyre Rock ward and was richly rewarded with a Flair. Quickly returning to Teptun's, Bloodgrue could not find the girl that stunned him. So he made a deal with old Blue Hair.*

Bloodgrue
By Rusty Knight
Episode thirteen, 'Lost'

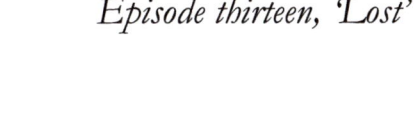

Bloodgrue
Volume 3: Business

We continue on …

Spring 42 Raccoon, Bloodgrue energetically rises from his bed. Looking out his small window at the souls twinkling in the sphere above, Bloodgrue ponders today. It is going to be another day like so many.

There is no light from the day-gods yet, yet it is hot already. The zephyr that inches across Bloodgrue's face indicates the gods barely breathe upon Quantos outside.

As usual, Bloodgrue lights his candle to start his day. He washes up then continues to the kitchen.

Having fed Master Onar, he then finishes script lessons.

With a few licks of dagger practice in, Bloodgrue then journeys out onto Willow Road. His target today is Teptun Square and Market where he will be looking for clients in this heat, which may prove to be a challenge.

Bloodgrue arrived over an hour ago and no one seems to need a Dragoman.

Well, except maybe the teenager who seems to be wandering aimlessly, looking lost.

Bloodgrue, tired of searching for a client, chances the possibility she needs help.

In trade jal he addresses the young jalfem. "Gods-grace and good fate, how do you fare young lady? You seem lost, may I help you?"

She stops and slowly turning she scowls. "I am lost, but I'm not sure I want help. Will it cost me anything?"

Bloodgrue visually and mentally sizes up her coin pouch before answering. "Normally I charge one Dyns a day, or one duster a kilometre, plus food and lodging. But, for you, I will make an exception. We can straighten up on the end of the journey, for a straight fee of one Dyns a day."

She extends her arm. "MY father will pay you."

Bloodgrue frowns, but then clasps arms. "What address are we looking for? And what is your name?"

The jalfem teenager huffs, but politely says. "My name is Allana; my father's house is at 3817 Derec Avenue, North Docks District. May we leave and head home today?"

Bloodgrue nods. "We may, is there anyone with you?"

Allana frowns then turning red she answers. "No, I ran away, but then got lost. I found myself here. But no one will help me."

Bloodgrue
Volume 3: Business

Bloodgrue waves her forward, starting the walk towards the south exit of Teptun's and out onto Fifth Street South Road, to head toward Derec Avenue.

Bloodgrue finds Allana walks slowly and the pair only covers about five and a half kilometres before gods-set. Looking for a safe place to bunk down for the night, he watches the sides of the road.

Walking in the near darkness, Bloodgrue notices a farmer's stable along the road with an open door.

"We stay here tonight and rise early to get a head start on the day tomorrow." Bloodgrue leads the way inside, going to the back looking for the straw manger.

Spring 43 Raccoon, the gods turn the world around, cooling it off drastically, putting a cover over Quantos in the sphere. Bloodgrue never noticed the time of day until it was late in the morning. Getting organized by nearly noon, the two of them sneak out the stable door without the farmer noticing.

Bloodgrue hurries Allana along Fifth Street South Road. They walk the whole day, using all of the light hours, but only covering another seven and a half kilometres. It is still a good long ways to Derec Avenue. Bloodgrue tried to devise a way to speed up Allana but nothing worked.

Near gods-set Bloodgrue finds an empty storage shed for the night's rest. Then the two wait for the next day to arrive.

Spring 44 Raccoon, it is nearly an hour after noon when they arrive at 3817 Derec Avenue.

Allana flings open the entry door and rushing past a flustered jalmal, she says. "You owe him some coins." As she points at Bloodgrue.

Storming off deeper into the house she leaves the two jalmals to deal with matters.

Bloodgrue decides to take the issues in hand. "Allana was lost. Is she your daughter?"

The man stunned, is shaking and confused, he nods while still trying to gather himself.

Bloodgrue continues. "I am Apprentice Dragoman Bloodgrue of 4212 Willow Road. I escorted Allana for three days to bring her home; my fee is one Dyns per day, plus food and lodging. So I am collecting six Dyns today for escorting Allana home."

Now really flabbergasted, the man stammers. "You expect … me t … pay that?"

Bloodgrue nods enigmatically. "Did you want her home?"

The man frowns deeply, and then taking his coin pouch off the side table beside him, he empties the entire contents of coins into his hand, offering them to Bloodgrue. "There you go. I have four Dyns and three dusters."

Bloodgrue hesitates, then taking the coins he returns one Dyns. "I will not leave a man coinless."

Bloodgrue extends his arm politely.

They clasp arms and Bloodgrue places the newly gathered coins into his coin pouch.

Bloodgrue confidently leaves the house.

He is making a much faster pace as he starts back towards Teptun Square and Market.

Spring 45 Raccoon, there is ice on the water in troughs and buckets this morning as the gods turn their breathing southward.

Bloodgrue has gone nearly nine kilometres in the time it took him and Allana to travel five.

Suddenly, a voice calls to him from the left. "Friend, could you help a man out? I am out of work and need some help … My family hasn't eaten in three days."

Bloodgrue turns to see who is addressing him. Sitting on a bench at the side of the road is a mature jalmal. Bloodgrue looks him over and smiles, as Bloodgrue notes the sigil tattooed on his wrist.

Signalling the sign that Luenen taught him for '*safe travel*', Bloodgrue watches the man curiously from a safe distance.

The man barely even registers seeing the sign. He continues to beg "Can you spare me a Dyns or a few dusters, Master? I am damn hungry and so is my family."

Bloodgrue frown and signs, '*Pandora*' while saying, "I might have a few coins for a friend. What name do you go by?"

The man blinks haphazardly while shifting on his seat. "They call me Andolf of Pandora, friend. A Dyns would help me out a lot."

Bloodgrue, contemplating this then replies. "I only have a few dusters myself, friend of Pandora."

Suddenly, Andolf has a club in hand and he says. "My eyes say your coin pouch can hold more than a few dusters friend and you look healthy enough to carry more than a few dusters. You don't wear the mark of Pandora. So don't be signing me and calling me friend"

Bloodgrue quickly decides to leave his dagger hidden. He's going to try negotiating his way out of this predicament.

"Friend, I am new Pandora, I am Blood of First Rank. I was at the house only recently talking with the master."

Andolf raises his club to waist height. "Hand me all of your coins, boy. No double talk. Any rogue can say those things. You need to be more specific to pass any test."

Bloodgrue raises his hands chest high and stands his ground. "Then if you know the rules of the house, you know if I get more specific I will be killed. But I think we can get past that. If you give me the door code, I will give you the response. Then we will know, we both know the house. I will then show you my mark. Fair trade?"

Andolf pauses for a minute, with his club getting heavier in his hand by the second. He stands, "Okay. What temple?"

Bloodgrue sighs, easing his muscles slightly. "Joyn of Lorn for Pandora. Now, I am going to show you my mark. It is in my coin pouch."

Slowly Bloodgrue reaches for his coin pouch. Loosening the draw strings, he reaches inside the pouch pulling out the marker, he shows it to Andolf. Then Bloodgrue quickly returns it back into his coin pouch. "May I see yours?"

Andolf pulls a cord with a small pouch from inside his worn tunic. From inside the pouch he produces an identical marker to Bloodgrue's. Then quickly he puts it away as a wagon team wanders by with a load. The drover greets the two and keeps going.

Andolf has put away his club, but he still glowers at Bloodgrue cautiously "Newbie. I still want coins. You can call it a toll to pass my station."

Bloodgrue ponders this, and then nods. He reaches into his pouch and pulls free two dusters. Drawing tight his coin pouch he then hands Andolf the two copper coins.

"Will these do?"

Andolf slips the coins secretly inside his tunic. "Don't forget. You pay a toll passing this station or I beat the feathers out of you. It is two dusters to pass every time boy."

Bloodgrue regrets stopping now, but he did. Doesn't mean he has to every time.

Spring 46 Raccoon, the gods are striking out at someone; they are breathing hard cold breaths west, breaking the cover in the sphere. It is late in the afternoon and Bloodgrue has been looking for a client for over an hour, with no luck. With the coins in his pouch from taking Allana home, Bloodgrue decides to go home and forget about more clients today.

Bloodgrue arrives at 4212 Willow Road with about four hours of day-gods light left and it feels odd. Walking into Onar's living area Bloodgrue opens his coin pouch and fishes out the three Dyns. He hands them to Onar. "I took home a run-away. She couldn't afford the full fee and then I got waylaid on the way back, loosing part of the fee."

Onar puts the coins aside, smiling. "So you are working well Bloodgrue. Another seven Dyns and you will have paid off the clothes. Let's go out to the courtyard and practice with the daggers, and then we will work script … Then, you will cook evening meal and eat with me."

Bloodgrue
Volume 3: Business

Bloodgrue smiles, Onar is in a good mood.

To be continued …

In the next episode fourteen, 'Client'

Bloodgrue settles a dispute between a freight-handler and farmer. Afterwards while enjoying an ale, an armourer asks Bloodgrue to deliver a package to the Mercenary Ward. Returning from the delivery Bloodgrue aids an old sailor home.

Bloodgrue
Volume 3: Business

Awesome! You finished an episode of '*Bloodgrue*'.

Let us know what you think of it by going to this this link: www.inupress.ca While you are there, you should join the Inevitable Unicorn Press e-mail subscription list to receive news and updates about work from our authors such as; Rusty Knight, Brian Hill and Aria. When you sign up for the e-mail list, you will receive a free pdf. This free pdf changes with time. In February 2016 the gift was a copy of Rusty Knight's biography of the protagonists, the Black Swans, from his novel, '*Laret*'. Later in 2016, the bonus is an issue from the serial series, '*Lanis*'.

While on the home page of InUPress.ca leave a comment telling us what you think of our author's work, or the website. We appreciate your time and we will respond to questions and comments.

Thank you for reading.
Yours,
Rusty Knight of Inevitable Unicorn Press.
www.inupress.ca

Bloodgrue
Volume 3: Business

Welcome to our serial stories!

If you're not familiar with our serial series, think of them as a favorite nighttime program that continues with a new episode each week, only this is in a book format. These are stories that don't necessarily have an end planned for them, or if they do, it's a long way off unlike many television series that we get interested in, only to have them go off air.

Serial stories are a great way to keep you entertained and on edge waiting to see what will happen next, in short enough episodes to enjoy on a lunch break, or before going to bed. Although our stories are designed to be read one episode per week, unlike TV stories, if you just can't wait for the next episode, you can get another one any time.

Be sure to download!

It is a good idea to download episodes when you first purchase them. Then, just read them at your leisure.

Please feel free to let us know what you think of our serial stories. It's a new trend and may take some getting used to, but we've had positive feedback in the past with them.

Now, it's time to enjoy!

InUPress

We would like to acknowledge the following for their work in the production of this series.

Cover design, C S Burgar
Editing, Donna Shumaker (Aria)

Bloodgrue
Volume 3: Business

Previously on *Bloodgrue* **Spring 42 Raccoon**, *Bloodgrue escorted home a lost jalfem teenager. He was waylaid on his way back to Teptun Square, losing part of his pay and being set a toll fee for using Fifth Street South Road by a Pandora thief who begs in the area.*

Bloodgrue
By Rusty Knight
Episode fourteen, 'Clients'

Bloodgrue
Volume 3: Business

We continue on …

Spring 51 Raccoon, in the strong east breaths of the gods, under the broken cover overhead in the sphere, Bloodgrue speaks with his client. "Master Dal. May you get a good price for your furs from your buyer here at the Lanky Maid ward. I'm not sure it's the best place for you to sell, but the merchant you asked for uses this shop. As you see, it's closed now."

The seventy-three-year-old jalmal frowns. Looking around he settles down his handcart. "Well, can you find me an inn until I find him open for business? I will pay your fee, plus a duster to get the inn."

Bloodgrue beams his grin. "Of course, follow me."

Bloodgrue leads Dal to the Sleeping Beauty Inn, at 327 Essec Avenue along the river.

Entering, Bloodgrue looks for Innkeeper Terrance. "Gods-grace and good fate, good-day Master Terrance. This is Trapper Dal. He has a cart with freight and needs a room and a place for safe keeping his cart with its goods."

Turning to Dal to speak, Bloodgrue is interrupted as Dal hands him one silver Dyns, and two copper dusters. "Thank you apprentice; your services are much appreciated. I think I can find the shop again in the morning. Gods-grace and good fate to you and yours."

Bloodgrue accepts the three coins and clasps arms with the man, parting ways satisfied.

Bloodgrue goes to the Lanky Maiden to drum up business. Entering the establishment at 24 Deer Street, Bloodgrue peers intently out among the patrons. Everyone seems to be busy drinking and Bloodgrue has two dusters to spend on such matters as well.

Bloodgrue takes a seat at the bar, so as to be free to approach. Bloodgrue waves over Barkeeper Lanna.

The fifty-seven-year old jalfem smiles, she comes over and cheerfully greets Bloodgrue. "What will it be Blood? Did you bring me customers?"

Bloodgrue sighs sadly. "Sorry, no customers, but a client tipped me enough for a half-pint of your dark ale. Anyone looking for a dragoman that you know of?"

Lanna slaps Bloodgrue's shoulder. "Pay for half, get a full pint. The last two you brought stayed the whole night and spent a Flair just in tips. Sorry, no clients for you either."

Bloodgrue hands Lanna the two dusters. Lanna walks around to her serving side of the bar and taps a pint of her best dark ale, serving it to Bloodgrue. She smiles and then continues to serve her other customers.

Bloodgrue continues to observe Lanna's customers.

Bloodgrue
Volume 3: Business

As the afternoon progresses, Bloodgrue overhears an argument next to him at the bar.

"I tell you the fee is fair. I told you fair upfront before unloading your wagon how much."

The seventy-plus-years-old jalfem farmer angrily replies. "You are charging me double the handling fees you quoted me to unload my grain. There is no way I can afford to pay your fees."

The dispute continues, with the old jalmal freight-handler saying. "My fee quote was up front, you miscalculated your load."

Bloodgrue, not one to leave disputes unsettled, offers to aid the two. "Excuse me. You have an issue. I am Apprentice Dragoman Bloodgrue of 4212 Willow road. I know I am a dragoman, but perhaps I can help you out. Perhaps, I can help you reach a settlement that you both can agree on?"

The farmer turns to Bloodgrue, smiling, and offers her arm to clasp. "Yes, a fresh mind would be appreciated. I accept your help Bloodgrue. I am Meridan. This is Darren. If he agrees, you can help settle our dispute."

Darren shrugs his shoulders non-committed. "I don't care, whatever. Just let's get this over with and pay me."

Bloodgrue clasps arms with an eager Meridan. Then he offers to clasp arms with Darren, which would make arbitration binding. The freight-handler hesitates; almost thirty seconds, then nods and clasps arms.

Bloodgrue moves aside his almost empty mug. "Okay, so from what I heard, the dispute is over fees for unloading grain from a wagon. Darren, tell me your part of this."

Darren huffs in disgust, and then he starts. "Meridan hired me to unload her sacks of grain at the 517 Essec Avenue warehouse, at two dusters a sack. I unloaded the sacks, counting forty-seven sacks, so she owes me ninety-four dusters. It is simple math."

Bloodgrue nods. Turning to Meridan he says calmly to her. "Meridan, tell me your side."

Meridan, almost sobbing, tells her story. "I asked him to unload my wagon of sacks of grain, yes. But there were not forty-seven. There were thirty on the manifest, that the warehouse paid me for. But he piled the sacks with a bunch of others and claims there were forty-seven, thus when I disputed it saying there were only thirty, I couldn't prove it by recount and he can't prove his by recount. Now he's trying to bully me into paying his desired fee."

Bloodgrue pauses, thinking. Then he asks Meridan. "So how much did the warehouse pay you for your grain?"

Meridan answers quickly. "Five dusters a sack for thirty sacks; fifteen Dyns, minus taxes of six percent, so a total of fourteen Dyns and seven dusters. So you see paying ninety-four dusters basically leaves me nothing."

Bloodgrue nods sagely, and answers. "True, and if they only paid you for thirty, either they only counted thirty, or they cheated you. Either way, you were counted thirty officially. That is the count. Master Darren wants paid for forty-seven sacks. I have an idea though. How large is the wagon, Master Darren?"

Darren perks up. "It was a medium, thousand-pound cargo wagon."

Bloodgrue asks Meridan. "Is this your answer as well?"

Meridan nods, "Yes."

Bloodgrue continues. "Meridan, what were the beasts of burden and their physical condition?"

Meridan, looking confused, answers. "Two mules in good health, fully fed and watered daily."

Bloodgrue asks Darren. "Did that appear true?"

Darren, also interested now, but confused. "Yes?"

Bloodgrue, serious, asks. "How full was the cargo box?

Meridan answers first. "Three-quarters."

Darren nods. "Yes, about three-quarters."

Bloodgrue starts calculating in his mind. Then he states his case to the two. "Okay, I know that a full grain sack is thirty-pounds. But let's say these sack are not full, say twenty-five pounds. The mules, being healthy, can pull the wagon full at one-thousand-pounds, so that is not an issue. You say three-quarters full. Let's give discrepancy and say slightly more than that, say eight-hundred-pounds of grain in the wagon. There is no way there could be forty-seven sacks of twenty-five pounds of grain in the wagon. At most there were thirty-two in the wagon. So if the warehouse counted thirty, that is likely accurate. Master Darren your count is obviously wrong. Master Meridan, only pay for thirty, at two dusters a sack. You owe Master Darren sixty dusters or six Dyns. Case settled. Master Darren, be more careful how you count."

Darren looks shocked at the result, knowing he has no way of arguing out of it. The facts worked out and the case was proven with facts. He looks at Meridan. "I accept. I think we each owe the judge two dusters as well, for a decent and fair judgement. No matter that I lost. I can't argue against him. He was fair and accurate."

Meridan looks at Darren, then taking her coin pouch from her belt she pays six Dyns to Darren and four dusters to Bloodgrue as she says to Darren. "Because you accepted so graciously, I agree on payment to the judge, and I will make your payment."

All three clasp arms with each other in acknowledgement, agreeing with the verdict.

Just as the acknowledgments are complete, an old jalmal taps Bloodgrue's shoulder. "Excuse me dragoman, the barkeep said you're for hire?"

Bloodgrue
Volume 3: Business

Bloodgrue, elated by events, nods and answers. "Yes … Yes, gods-grace and good fate, how may I be of service to you master?"

The old jalmal replies. "I have to deliver some armour to the Fish Market in Lance's Mercenary ward. Can you help me get it there? Can you take it to stall 12 for me?"

Bloodgrue nods, a courier job. A few are good, and are a set fee. "Three Dyns Master, and I will deliver your package. I will leave tomorrow morning. I will be staying tonight in the Sleeping Beauty, if you can have the package there and ready tonight, I leave well before gods-rise."

"I am Armourer Tess and it's a repaired, plate helm for mercenary Eri, if you can get it to him. He has already paid me, so you have no need to collect. I will have it and your fee, to you, within the hour. Thank you." He departs quickly after clasping arms.

Bloodgrue drains his dark ale and walks to the Sleeping Beauty for the night.

Spring 52 Raccoon, is starting out bad, with rain and it is not a light rain. The package Armourer Tess delivered to Bloodgrue is ten pounds, and it is bulky. The heat has built before the gods have even breached the horizon; they breathe strongly driving the rains hard into Bloodgrue's back.

Spring 53 Raccoon, nearing evening, the cold air drove Bloodgrue on strongly today. Stall 12 is a mercenary for hire that Bloodgrue believes will likely be hungry for some time until he cleans up.

Dock A of the Fish Market, in Lance's Mercenary ward is a mix of merchants and mercenaries for hire. Bloodgrue's stomach curdles here, as he walks among the cut-throats. But he was paid well and over the years he has made enough trips in to learn the area.

As Bloodgrue is exiting, a sailor calls to him in jal. "Gods-grace and good fate, do you have a moment lad?"

Bloodgrue turns to see a nearly century-old jalfem walking the sea-walk towards him from the side of the street.

Bloodgrue concedes. "Of course I have time for you. Gods-grace and good fate, how may I be of service master?"

The jalfem stops ten-feet from Bloodgrue, glassy eyed she whispers. "I'm lost, lad."

Bloodgrue nods, seeing this to be a common issue among the old and young. "Where do you live Pampamoo and what is your name?"

The old jalfem beams happily. "I am Sailor Angamor from the Dew Drop Host tavern in Stonewire's Pier ward. Do you think you can help?"

Bloodgrue extends his arm to clasp. "For six dusters, Pampamoo Angamor I will get you home."

Almost before he finishes speaking she has clasped his arm.

Angamor adds. "I think this late we should stay at that inn. Over there; for the night and start tomorrow."

Bloodgrue, understanding how distressed Angamor must be, answers her calmly. "Yes, Pampamoo, we can stay there. That is the Mighty Inn; we will stay there tonight and leave before gods-rise tomorrow, okay? It should only take us a few hours walking tomorrow to get you home. Fear not you're safe."

She grins and takes Bloodgrue's elbow. "Thank you lad, let's go."

Spring 54 Raccoon, they had to find Pampamoo Angamor a better cloak, as it has gotten colder today.

Arriving in mid-afternoon, at the Dew Drop Host on 246 Teptun West Street, Bloodgrue quickly locates Barkeep Alana. "Gods-grace and good fate Alana, is Sailor Angamor your Pampamoo?"

Alana shrieks hysterically in excitement. "You found her? Where?"

Bloodgrue smiles as he is being hugged. He replies. "Yes, she was in the mercenary ward. She is fine. Your pampamoo paid the six duster dragoman fee, but I kind of feel guilty. Not enough to return the fee, as I have to eat too, and it is my work. But I suggest keeping a closer eye on her, and I will keep an eye out as well. The next return will be free; she is a delight to talk with. Take care now."

Alana takes Bloodgrue's hand and places two dusters in it, while smiling. "Thank you, dragoman."

Bloodgrue shrugs, and he nods. "You're welcome."

Exiting, he starts walking for home.

Spring 56 Raccoon, the ice beat on Bloodgrue the whole walk today, until he reached home at 4212 Willow Road. Entering the building, Bloodgrue is shivering violently.

Taking off his cloak, he hangs it on his hook and he walks into Onar's living area. Bloodgrue finds Onar sitting by a blazing fire. Onar motions to a seat close to the fire. "Sit and dry off. Looks like you need to warm up as well."

Bloodgrue sits on the offered seat, the warmth of the fire burning into him. He starts to fumble with the cords of his coin pouch. Onar taps Bloodgrue's hands. "Wait till your hands thaw boy. No need to rush ... you have a message ... a Noah, from Western Madison requests your presence for a business matter. Says it's urgent. I received the message two days ago. You can go tomorrow, if you're not sick."

Bloodgrue's hands soon warm up. He is able to pay Onar another four Dyns and six dusters in fees he collected, for Onar's dues.

Bloodgrue
Volume 3: Business

To be continued …

In the next episode fifteen, '*Noah Summons Bloodgrue*'

In Western Madison a woman beat a boy breaking his arm, Bloodgrue judges her with Noah's aid. In the court Noah and Bloodgrue also handle a case of a landlord who wants to raise the rent on his tenant before the renewal term of their contract, Bloodgrue conducts arbitration along with Noah, between the parties.

Bloodgrue
Volume 3: Business

Awesome! You finished an episode of '*Bloodgrue*'.

Let us know what you think of it by going to this this link: www.inupress.ca While you are there, you should join the Inevitable Unicorn Press e-mail subscription list to receive news and updates about work from our authors such as; Rusty Knight, Brian Hill and Aria. When you sign up for the e-mail list, you will receive a free pdf. This free pdf changes with time. In February 2016 the gift was a copy of Rusty Knight's biography of the protagonists, the Black Swans, from his novel, '*Laret*'. Later in 2016, the bonus is an issue from the serial series, '*Lanis*'.

While on the home page of InUPress.ca leave a comment telling us what you think of our author's work, or the website. We appreciate your time and we will respond to questions and comments.

Thank you for reading.
Yours,
Rusty Knight of Inevitable Unicorn Press.
www.inupress.ca

Bloodgrue
Volume 3: Business

Welcome to our serial stories!

If you're not familiar with our serial series, think of them as a favorite nighttime program that continues with a new episode each week, only this is in a book format. These are stories that don't necessarily have an end planned for them, or if they do, it's a long way off unlike many television series that we get interested in, only to have them go off air.

Serial stories are a great way to keep you entertained and on edge waiting to see what will happen next, in short enough episodes to enjoy on a lunch break, or before going to bed. Although our stories are designed to be read one episode per week, unlike TV stories, if you just can't wait for the next episode, you can get another one any time.

Be sure to download!

It is a good idea to download episodes when you first purchase them. Then, just read them at your leisure.

Please feel free to let us know what you think of our serial stories. It's a new trend and may take some getting used to, but we've had positive feedback in the past with them.

Now, it's time to enjoy!

InUPress

We would like to acknowledge the following for their work in the production of this series.

Cover design, C S Burgar
Editing, Donna Shumaker (Aria)

Bloodgrue
Volume 3: Business

Previously on *Bloodgrue* **Spring 51 Raccoon**, *Bloodgrue escorted a trapper from Low Tide ward into Lanky Maid ward. Later as he was on his way out drumming up business in the Lanky Maiden, Bloodgrue settled a dispute between a farmer and a freight-handler, for which Bloodgrue was rewarded. Afterwards, he received a courier contract from an armourer, to take a helm into the mercenary ward. As Bloodgrue is leaving the delivery he discovers a lost sailor. Taking her to her home, Bloodgrue is reward by her family. Finally home going to 4212 Willow, rewarded and frozen, Bloodgrue receives an urgent summons by peasant-hero Noah into Western Madison ward.*

Bloodgrue
By Rusty Knight
Episode fifteen, 'Noah Summons Bloodgrue'

Bloodgrue
Volume 3: Business

We continue on …

Spring 57 Raccoon, leaving on 4212 Willow Road in the heat of darkness is not new, but the demand is. The summons was urgent, Noah never summoned Bloodgrue before. The summons is three days old now.

Bloodgrue has to give himself time though, to arrive at Fifth Avenue at gods-rise. It takes just over two-hours to walk the almost three-kilometres from 4212 Willow Road, to the intersection of Oak Street and Fifth Avenue. The broken cover in the sphere is making it hard to judge time, but Bloodgrue thinks there are two-hours to gods-rise.

Bloodgrue brought his short-sword with him strapped on, his dagger hidden in its place. Ten dusters are in his coin pouch. He is wearing his Western Madison clothes, made by Guilda, and his attitude.

Arriving before gods-rise at his first destination, Bloodgrue waits. He waits nearly twenty-minutes before the yellow-god Stonewire and the red/orange-god Imvor break the eastern horizon. Seeing the scattered beams of red, orange and yellow light sneak through the broken cover in the sphere, Bloodgrue walks forward fifteen metres onto Fifth Avenue.

Standing with his hands away from his sword and his hands open, not in fists, Bloodgrue shouts out clearly in toy. "Honey, I'm home. Where's the ale?"

He only has to wait ten-minutes before two jovial toyfems of about twenty-years-age, come out of the buildings. Bloodgrue recognizes both Wardens and smiles. He waits silently for them to acknowledge him.

Gretch taps his arm and states. "You shouldn't be wearing a sword Blood … But as you are on duty it will be allowed today. Noah's anxious and been waiting … so don't delay much longer. He is at Red Square waiting for your arrival."

Bloodgrue nods, now knowing why he was summoned. It is for Western Madison Justice court duty, the second session. "Thank you Gretch. I will go straight to Red Square … Don't worry, I've learned enough to use the sword safely, I won't accidently hurt anyone."

The two women clasp arms with Bloodgrue, and then they go back into the buildings, as Bloodgrue walks along the centre of Fifth Avenue. Bloodgrue walks quickly the full two-and-a-half-kilometres to Red Square, at number 2, Fifth Avenue and Lively Street.

Entering the tavern, Bloodgrue finds it nearly empty, except for a grumpy appearing Noah, sitting alone at the back table, and a nervous appearing Willa, who is cleaning the tavern's fixtures.

Bloodgrue sees this scene. He shouts boisterously. "Hey, have you beaten any jalnoric tradesmen lately, dog meat?"

Noah jumps up from his seat, nearly spilling over his table. Rushing over, cheerfully excited, as two armed women rush out of room three, ready to fight. Noah tightly embraces Bloodgrue, who returns the hug while Bloodgrue says. "It's nice to be here and see you too, dog meat."

Bloodgrue
Volume 3: Business

Settling down, Noah says. "We have court, one bad one and one dispute. Come on … WILLA, a round of drinks for the four of us. You can have one to if you want."

Together, the two friends walk to the table that is designated as Noah's. He waves his two enforcers over to join them, signalling for them to stand down.

Willa sets the four drinks on the table and addresses Noah. "Can I reserve mine for after work?"

Noah blinks apologetically. "Yes, and take tomorrow off with pay. Have your sister cover for you if you think she can."

Willa beams a wide grin. "You're the best boss. She will be here. I will have my drink tomorrow night then, if you're fine with that, Boss?"

Noah nods. "Yes, Sweet-heart, of course. Now go and leave us be in peace for a bit."

Willa returns to cleaning the tavern with renewed vigor, and beaming a new grin.

The four at Noah's table drink and talk for a few minutes, then Noah sends an enforcer to get Councilman Tot and the two cases for court, to be held in two hours.

…..

Councilman Tot brought the defendants, accusers and witnesses for both cases to Red Square, on time. Word got out quickly, and Red Square is full, standing room is taken up by as many as can fill the tavern. People are standing outside. The two enforcers are holding an area around Noah and Bloodgrue's table for the court proceedings to take place. An area ten-by-fifteen-feet around Noah's table, set in front of the door to room three.

Sitting at the table, Noah and Bloodgrue are nearly overwhelmed by the response to the court.

Standing as primary judge, Noah speaks first. "Councilman Tot, we are ready to open the First Justice Court of Western Madison, second session. Please bring forth the first case." Noah sits again.

Councilman Tot leads forth a toyfem of about forty-years in appearance. "Judges of the court, we bring to you a case of assault. This is Gellea of Western Madison ward. She is found accused of severely beating her son Genner, who is seven-years-old. She beat him until breaking his right arm and continued to beat him. You, yourself Master Noah, fetched the mid-wife to set young Genner's arm and paid the fees. We have three witnesses to the beating; you may examine them at your discretion."

Noah and Bloodgrue nod.

Bloodgrue speaks first. "Where is Genner now?"

Bloodgrue
Volume 3: Business

Councilman Tot answers directly. "We have asked that Genner stay with his pampamoo until the court decides this case. She agreed on the short term, but asked that he not stay with her long term. She is getting on in years."

Bloodgrue acknowledges Tot with a nod. "Okay Gellea, first, I would like to hear your statement."

Gellea grunts in disdain. "What it matter? You have no authority here. This a bunch of dog dropping show. Genner was being a boy and bad. I kick his ass and tell him to get good. Simple. It no one else's business. He be fine."

Noah lets out a small disgruntled sigh. Then he instructs Tot. "Your first witness is Terri. Please bring him forward."

Councilman Tot waves forward a ten-year-old boy. The boy hesitates, then while watching the floor, red faced, he cautiously steps up to the table.

Bloodgrue begins with an opening question. "What's your name, lad?"

The boy briefly looks up. "Like he said; my name's Terri."

Bloodgrue asks. "Do you know Genner very well?"

Terri nods and answers. "He's my best friend; we play together all the time. His mama doesn't like me."

Gellea coughs and blurts out. "That aint so boy."

Bloodgrue holds up his hand and looks at Gellea shaking his head. "No speaking, unless directed to."

Turning back to Terri, Bloodgrue continues. "Did you see Gellea beat Genner? Did you see her break his arm?"

Terri cringes slightly, hesitating, he answers slowly. "She beats him a lot, and yes, I saw her beating him that time. She hit him with a stick, a bunch of times. He was crying, and she kept hitting him saying, shut up."

Noah nods and says, "Thank you Terri, you can step away now … Councilman Tot, your next witness."

Tot waves forth a very old toymal.

The pampaloo stands in front of the table, bent over with age. Bloodgrue asks the man "What is your name, Pampaloo?"

The old man gargles out. "My name is Lener."

Noah asks the next question. "How are you involved in this?"

Lener tries to straighten taller. "I was walking by, when I saw the woman beating the boy with a stick … while he was crying. I tried to stop her. She beat him until he was quiet … I couldn't stop her."

Bloodgrue asks. "And this is the woman?"

Lener looks over at Gellea, then back to Bloodgrue. "Absolutely, I recognize her and the hate is still in her eyes."

"Okay, thank you Pampaloo Lener, you may step back." Offers Noah.

Bloodgrue gestures towards Tot. "Next."

Councilman Tot motions to a middle-aged toymal, who boldly steps up to the table and confidently waits.

Bloodgrue addresses him. "Master, your name and involvement please."

The man grins angrily. "Of course, I am Lance. As to my involvement, I got to the scene as she was beating a little boy unconscious with a stick. I picked the boy up and brought him to someone who would know what to do, and do it. I brought him to Red Square, and our man, Noah here. Noah had me go get the mid–wife, to check over Genner and set the boy's broken arm. Noah, being a man, also paid the mid–wife, as I was unable to. I have to support my family on the meagre income I am able to make. A better man you won't find than Master Noah. A worse woman, than Gellea as a mother, you won't find. If anyone beat one of my boys like she beat hers, they wouldn't be walking again."

Bloodgrue nods, pointing to Gellea. "And that woman, is the same woman, you are sure?"

Lance looks over at Gellea, and then back at Noah and Bloodgrue. "Sure as there are Seven Hells, I am sure."

Noah waves him off politely. "Okay, thank you Lance. Councilman Tot, anymore witnesses?"

Tot shakes his head, answering firmly. "None, judges."

Noah stands, as does Bloodgrue. Noah speaks to those in the room. "Thank you, we will be back shortly."

The two enter room three, with Bloodgrue closing the door.

Noah shivers. "That woman is evil, Blood. This is not the first time she beat Genner senseless."

Bloodgrue sighs sadly and deeply. "She is guilty; we can't argue otherwise. Law of the Dominnion says flogging is punishment, or goal time. We don't have a goal, which I am aware of."

Bloodgrue
Volume 3: Business

Noah sits down. "The council has a goal, with three cells. But they would be wasted on her. How much flogging can we do?"

Bloodgrue answers uncertainly, "I think, if I remember right, Onar said from twenty, up to one-hundred. It depends on the severity of the crime, and number of repeat offenses by the offender. I think she deserves at least twenty, if not fifty."

Noah growls, "OK, fifty and it will be my pleasure to be the whip man. Let's do this."

Noah calms himself, and then he stands.

They go out into the court room.

Standing together at their table, Noah addresses the room. "Okay everyone, you heard as well as we did, the witnesses identified Gellea as the one in question, and the savagery with which she beat her son. We decided on her case. First she is guilty. Now, her punishment is flogging of fifty lashes carried out at gods-rise tomorrow, by me here at the Red Square. She will be held in the Council's goal until then. She also loses Genner permanently. He goes to Wilma Nora, who you know is my mother and curses me every day that I live here, and Wilma Nora will love and adore Genner. Right, mama, I see you there along the wall. Is it yes, or no … Wilma Nora?"

A gruff female voice calls out. "Yes … you scoundrel."

Bloodgrue says even-toned. "Case settled. Next case Councilman Tot."

Councilman Tot stands forth and proclaims the next case. "This is a dispute between Landlord Teerk and the Formic Family. Teerk desires to increase the rent on the property. The Formic's declare abuse, stating they cannot afford the increase and will have to move. Their contract is binding still for five more years, but Teerk wants the increase now, stating they can afford the increase, as another family member has become employed in a trade."

Bloodgrue looks over the group, as he is thinking; so does Noah.

Bloodgrue breaks the ice. "Master Teerk, please state your case."

The sixty-seven-year-old toymal stands before the table. "For years I have had these people as tenants in this house. I have looked after the house and paid taxes. Now that they are all employed, am I not entitled to a fair compensation and income from my property? They pay two dusters a square foot per season now. I am asking for it to be increased to three dusters a square foot per season."

Bloodgrue nods, "Okay, master of the Formics. Please step forward, and state your case."

A middle-aged toyfem steps forward to stand besides Teerk. "Gods-grace and good fate master judges. We ask that this not happen, as we can barely afford the rent and to eat now, with all four of us working. An increase in rent and we will need to move from out home of over thirty years."

Noah asks Teerk. "State the size of the abode."

Teerk offers quickly. "The building is thirty-feet by thirty-feet and two-stories."

Noah turns to the toyfem. "Meada, is this correct?"

She replies. "Yes, it is."

Bloodgrue asks. "And how is it built? Is it all wood? Is it slate, or thatch roof?"

Meada answers. "All wood, with a thatch roof."

Teerk nods. "Yes, she is right."

Bloodgrue turns to Meada. "Does Teerk keep it up? What condition is it in?"

Meada frowns and grimacing, she answers. "It is in fair condition, like any in the ward."

Bloodgrue nods. "Okay, that brings up your condition Meada. What are your wages, and what work does your family do?"

She hesitates, and then answers confidently, though not bragging. "Everet, my life-companion, he is a labouring Sailor. He earns one Dyns a day from his Captain. I work repairing barges in Terrington Mors, for three Dyns a day. My boy Kruen works in Sterric ward for Villein Kruppa, as a farm labourer for three dusters a day. Leopor, my youngest, just got taken on as apprentice carpenter, with Master Tomek. Master Tomek generously pays one duster per day."

Noah smiles, and he enquires. "Do you have any other income, Meada?"

The matron shakes her head slowly. "No, we have none."

Bloodgrue stands and addresses the room. "Ok, we are taking a moment. We will be back soon."

The two boys retire to room three. Noah closes the door. Bloodgrue sits at the table, with the chalk he found, he works out the math on the table surface.

Looking at Noah, he sighs. "They are right. They can't afford a rent increase … Look here. They have a daily income of forty-four dusters among the four of them, when they all work. The house is eighteen-hundred square feet. Currently, they pay forty-dusters a day rent. If we let him increase the rent to three-dusters per square foot, that increases their rent to sixty-dusters per day. They can never afford that. Let's lock them in for another fifteen years at two dusters."

Noah looks at Bloodgrue quizzically. "Where did you learn that Blood? I can do figures in my head roughly, but that is sheer brain work and this on the table means nothing to me. Teach me, ok dog beater?"

Bloodgrue sits back, and then smiles. "Okay, if you agree to a fifteen-year lock-in."

Bloodgrue
Volume 3: Business

Noah extends his arm. "Done!"

Noah and Bloodgrue are standing in the tavern with their audience; with the two looking at the defendants.

Noah turns to Bloodgrue and bows. "It is all yours, brains."

Bloodgrue addresses the audience. "It appears that the Formics are correct. As it stands, their income, when all four are working is forty-four dusters a day. Their current rent is forty dusters per day, leaving them four dusters a day to live on, if all four work, every day. Now, Landlord Teerk wants to increase rent to three dusters per square foot. Which means the rent will be sixty dusters per day. The Formics will be short sixteen dusters every day even if they all work every day. We are denying the rent increase and locking the rent in at two dusters per square foot per season, for fifteen years. The case is settled. Thus we are closing the second session of the First Justice Court of Western Madison. Drink up, or get the Seven Hells out. We need room to breathe."

Noah stands and shouts. "I second that, and one round is on the house. You have fifteen minutes to claim your free drink. Or, come to me for a chit to claim a free drink later tonight."

To be continued …

In the next episode sixteen, '*Run for Pampaloo Ottar*'

We find Bloodgrue summoned by Pampaloo Ottar, who sends Bloodgrue on a run. On the run Bloodgrue encounters Andolf again and has to deal with the beggar. During this run, Bloodgrue discovers Annelee and they strike up an odd relationship that they carry back to Pampaloo Ottar's.

Bloodgrue
Volume 3: Business

Awesome! You finished an episode of '*Bloodgrue*'.

Let us know what you think of it by going to this this link: www.inupress.ca While you are there, you should join the Inevitable Unicorn Press e-mail subscription list to receive news and updates about work from our authors such as; Rusty Knight, Brian Hill and Aria. When you sign up for the e-mail list, you will receive a free pdf. This free pdf changes with time. In February 2016 the gift was a copy of Rusty Knight's biography of the protagonists, the Black Swans, from his novel, '*Laret*'. Later in 2016, the bonus is an issue from the serial series, '*Lanis*'.

While on the home page of InUPress.ca leave a comment telling us what you think of our author's work, or the website. We appreciate your time and we will respond to questions and comments.

Thank you for reading.
Yours,
Rusty Knight of Inevitable Unicorn Press.
www.inupress.ca

Bloodgrue
Volume 3: Business

Welcome to our serial stories!

If you're not familiar with our serial series, think of them as a favorite nighttime program that continues with a new episode each week, only this is in a book format. These are stories that don't necessarily have an end planned for them, or if they do, it's a long way off unlike many television series that we get interested in, only to have them go off air.

Serial stories are a great way to keep you entertained and on edge waiting to see what will happen next, in short enough episodes to enjoy on a lunch break, or before going to bed. Although our stories are designed to be read one episode per week, unlike TV stories, if you just can't wait for the next episode, you can get another one any time.

Be sure to download!

It is a good idea to download episodes when you first purchase them. Then, just read them at your leisure.

Please feel free to let us know what you think of our serial stories. It's a new trend and may take some getting used to, but we've had positive feedback in the past with them.

Now, it's time to enjoy!

InUPress

We would like to acknowledge the following for their work in the production of this series.

Cover design, C S Burgar
Editing, Donna Shumaker (Aria)

Bloodgrue
Volume 3: Business

Previously on *Bloodgrue* **Spring 57 Raccoon**, *Noah summoned Bloodgrue to court where they ordered a woman flogged for beating her seven-year-old son senseless, breaking his arm. The second case was a landlord wanting to instill a rent increase on his tenant family, because their son was taken on as a trade apprentice. The court instead locked in the current rent for fifteen years to protect the family.*

Bloodgrue
By Rusty Knight

Episode sixteen, 'Run for Pampaloo Ottar'

Bloodgrue
Volume 3: Business

We continue on …

Spring 64 Raccoon, the god's breath is howling eastward, as Bloodgrue is practicing his short-sword skills with Onar in the twilight of the day, when a client enters the courtyard, she looks around and approaches the two.

In jal she speaks. "Excuse me, I seek Dragoman Bloodgrue."

Bloodgrue sheaths his short-sword and responds. "I am Apprentice Dragoman Bloodgrue. Gods-grace and good fate, how may I be of service?"

The jalfem nods. "Gods-grace and good fate Dragoman Bloodgrue. I have a message from Master Ottar Marrel. He is in need of your service, as soon as you can arrive at his residence, for a service run south. That is all."

Bloodgrue nods while smiling happily. Digging his hand into his coin pouch, he pulls out one of the three remaining dusters and gives it to the messenger. "Thank you. I will be there tomorrow. No need to inform, Ottar, as I will likely arrive when you will."

The messenger leaves, and Onar approaches. "This is good; you have more regular clients. Be good to them and honest, Blood, and I will look after you as well."

Spring 65 Raccoon, the freezing ice from the night has Bloodgrue slowed down on his walk to Ottar's. Arriving in the afternoon, knocking on the door, Bloodgrue waits in the scattered shafts of god's light.

Ottar eventually arrives at the door, opening it he grins. "Come in Blood, nice to see you boy. Let's have some soup."

Bloodgrue enters 3237 Fifth Street South Road, into the hallway, following Ottar to the kitchen. Entering the kitchen, there is a short thirty-year-old jalmal. He stands at about five-foot-six and nearly 250 pound.

Bloodgrue wonders how he walks far.

Ottar points to the man. "Dragoman Bloodgrue, this is my client, Labourer Mel, a good gambling client who has amassed a small fortune, gaming with me, and he has asked for my help."

Mel is turning red and stammering. He looks at Ottar. "You … you go… oing to tr … trust him?"

Ottar calmly looks at Mel. "I trust Bloodgrue with all my high runs. He has never lost one on me ever. This run he can do in his sleep."

Turning to Bloodgrue, Ottar fills him in. "We need you to deposit fifty Flairs for Mel into Heran Usury. Do you mind?"

Bloodgrue
Volume 3: Business

Bloodgrue shrugs. "Do you have the expense pouch? I got targeted last run, by a Pandora, for a toll. I might have to pay him."

Ottar reaches for a shelf. "Ten as usual, use it to pay the toll, Blood."

Bloodgrue accepts the heavy leather coin pouch, adding it with his. "Ok, and the pack?"

Ottar places three bowls of soup on the table and three ales. "After the soup, Blood. It's by the door. It is the usual one."

Bloodgrue smiles at Ottar, as he enjoys Ottar's cooking, recalling that Ottar is a chef. Sitting at the table, Bloodgrue waits for the other two before digging in. Then politely, using the etiquette Ottar is teaching him, Bloodgrue eats the soup and drinks the ale. Bloodgrue finishes eating first, then waits until the other two finish.

"May I please be excused Master Ottar, so I will get under way. I should be only four days, barring weather or incident."

Mel looks shocked. "You can make it to Heran and back in four days? No way. I will put two Flairs against that. There is no way you will be back in four days, Bloodgrue."

Bloodgrue smiles confidently. "Master Ottar, will you back me on this?"

Ottar smiles confidently. "I've seen you do it, but you were exhausted. Let's say five. Mel, you can stay here five days. If Blood isn't back in five days, I will pay up two Flairs, on Blood's behalf which he will owe to me." The three clasp arms in a binding agreement.

Bloodgrue barely gets eighty metres down Fifth Street South Road, when he spots Andolf sitting watching Bloodgrue. There is no way around the man or past him unseen now. The man signs Bloodgrue. *'tithe'*

'damn seven hells' thinks Bloodgrue.

Walking casually over, Bloodgrue drops a Dyns in the bowl, from Ottar's pouch. Hastily, Andolf grabs Bloodgrue's wrist and utters in course jal. "Pretty rich for one who claims poor apprentice, your fee just went up. You owe a Dyns to pass my station. Don't forget."

He lets go of Bloodgrue's wrist roughly, growling at Bloodgrue. He pats his club that sits on the bench beside him.

Bloodgrue shrugs and replies. "We will see Andolf. We will see." Bloodgrue pats his short-sword strapped at his waist, winking at Andolf.

Bloodgrue walks away without further confrontation and Andolf proceeds no further, having gained his Dyns.

Near gods-set, Bloodgrue finds an open stable to lie down in for the night. Wrapping his cloak around him for the warmth it provides against the freezing day, Bloodgrue goes to sleep.

Bloodgrue
Volume 3: Business

Spring 66 Raccoon, finds Bloodgrue awake very early and up on the road in still freezing conditions. In the darkness of early morning the partial cloud cover obscures the surroundings somewhat, making Bloodgrue nervous, but he travels quicker hoping to avoid any confrontations.

Walking along on Derec Street, nearly to Heran Usury, Bloodgrue feels the tug.

Faster than he ever recalls reacting in his life, he spins and pulls his dagger. Catching the wrist with one hand and his dagger in his other hand, he looks at an old jalfem. She is average height and light, plain looking, she could be any child's pampamoo.

Bloodgrue asks carefully. "Guild"

She signs back, 'rolain'

Bloodgrue lets go of her arm, knowing she is out of her territory.

"Pampamoo, what the seven hells are you doing here? You just tried to take my client's deposit. I would end up in a very deep well with no way out. You are in a deep pile now yourself. You are in Pandora territory you know."

The old woman frowns sadly. "Pickens are getting light at home. I got known. I have to transfer out."

Bloodgrue takes a quick look at her hands to confirm she still has both. Then he nods. "You're rough. I am bad at detecting and I felt you. What's your prime skill?"

She shakes her head sadly. "I'm getting old and losing my hands. The pockets are my prime. I'm Annelee; I'm Fifth Rank in Rolain. Got passed over for lieutenant, so trying to make my way, but my hands aren't what they used to be. My mind's still good though. You're not going to turn me into the Watch?"

Bloodgrue is only sixteen, but he has an idea. He smiles and extends his arm to clasp while he says. "You will travel with me Pampamoo Annelee. I won't turn you in. I will put your mind to work and take you off the road if my friend will agree. But it will cost you five Dyns here and now, or you are back on your own and I report you to the local Pandora Wardens."

Annelee looks confused. She stands there a few seconds. Then she extends her arm and clasps and releases the grip.

Bloodgrue smiles and stands silently waiting.

Suddenly it dawns on Annelee and she opens her pouch, taking out five Dyns she hands them to Bloodgrue. "So, do I call you my Master now?"

Bloodgrue puts the five silver coins in his pouch, shaking his head. "No, you might be calling my friend Luenen, Master soon though. I am making a deposit, then we are going north. You and I."

"Okay, where can we eat though?" asks Annelee.

Bloodgrue digs in his backpack and then hands her a piece of his hard tack and his water-skin. "This will do for now."

Together they walk the last fifteen minutes to Heran Usury.

Bloodgrue stops outside the building. "Wait out here and be here when I come out. I am your friend now."

Entering the dressed-stone building at 3715 Derec Avenue, Bloodgrue peers around the room, searching for the middle-aged jalmal he knows so well. Bloodgrue spots the handsome man at his desk and walks over. "Gods-grace and good fate Master Heran. May I impose upon you?"

Looking up quickly and beaming a huge smile, Heran stands and extends his arm. "Apprentice Bloodgrue, gods-grace and good fate, how do you fare my friend? You making use of the slate I gave you? Do you need a second one?"

Bloodgrue chuckles and enthusiastically clasps arms with Heran. "Master Heran, gladly a second slate and more chalk. I will pay for them, my friend. I am actually here on business again. This is strictly a client's deposit."

Sitting down, Heran gestures to a seat. Smiling cheerfully, he instructs. "Please sit and let's do the work. The chalk is a duster for five sticks. The slate, if you are fine with the one I gave you is free, Blood."

Bloodgrue plops the deposit bag on the desk and says. "Okay then, another slate the same, plus a Dyns worth of chalk please. So I have here Fifty Flairs for Mel. There is the note with all of his information. He is a customer of Ottar Marrel if you need more."

Heran nods and looking at the bag, asks. "Did you confirm the coins?"

Bloodgrue smiles mischievously. "No, I thought we could do that together."

The two men confirm fifty Flairs in the bag. Heran makes out the deposit slip and gets Bloodgrue a slate and a Dyns worth of chalk. The two clasp arms completing their business.

Stepping outside, Bloodgrue finds Annelee sitting and waiting for him. He reaches for his water-skin. Finding it empty, he frowns and enters the usury again getting it filled.

Meeting up with Annelee again, now with a full water-skin, Bloodgrue looks her over. "You can walk just fine, so let's go. You are rested and I have to be back to my client in two days. Let's move."

The two walk for three hours. Then after gods-set, Bloodgrue spots a farm he knows somewhat.

Knocking on the house door, when the jalmal answers, Bloodgrue enquires. "Gods-grace and good fate master, we are traveling to the docks and I was wondering if we could trouble you to rent us a room and sell us some food and ale, much as I did last time?"

The middle-aged farmer nods. "Gods-grace and good fate, you were well behaved last time, so I see no harm, come on in. Four dusters for the room and nine dusters will get the two of you a hot meal and some ale. Fair enough Dragoman?"

Bloodgrue smiles easily. "I may stop here on more trips, at those prices, if you allow it my friend. I will pay now and we will leave before gods-rise. So no morning meals are needed. But a hot meal is most appreciated tonight. This is Annelee, my client I am taking to the docks. She has a job she is going to there, that I located for her."

The farmer clasps arms with Bloodgrue then Annelee. "Gods-grace and good fate Master Annelee, may fortune favour you in your new job. This dragoman seems to help a lot of people. Travel safe tomorrow, I hope you have good weather."

Annelee smiles for the farmer. "I too hope I have good fortune, and I think the weather will be fine. Thank you for your kindness."

Spring 68 Raccoon, Bloodgrue looks at Andolf sternly, "So you insist on one Dyns for Pandora, every time I pass by this place?"

Bloodgrue looks at Annelee as Andolf snarls a reply. "Yes, that is the fee for you to pass this way boy."

Bloodgrue pays the Dyns from Ottar's expense pouch.

The pair continues their walk.

Bloodgrue says to Annelee when they are more than fifty metres away. "You will witness that for me, when I ask you to?"

Annelee, looking confused, replies. "You actually want me to confess, to you having to pay a toll to a beggar there?"

Bloodgrue nods. "Yes, when I ask you to. You will earn your job doing so."

Bloodgrue knocks on the door at 3237 Fifth Street South Road. It is half-an-hour past noon on day four since picking up the deposit pack.

The door opens and Bloodgrue grins. "I think I earned my two Flairs, don't you?"

Pampaloo Ottar bursts out laughing. "You broke your previous record dragoman. You will sleep well for a night or two. Come in. I see you brought someone with you. Let's feed you two. I'll get Mel. You have the slip?"

"In the pack. Master Ottar Marrel this is Master Annelee. I am escorting her to a new job in Morelock Docks ward. I would appreciate if we could rent rooms from you tonight. Both of us are exhausted from two days of forced travel."

Ottar extends his arm to Annelee. "Come in, eat up and spend the night. I would enjoy some more company, with you two."

The two clasp arms.

In the kitchen Mel looks flabbergasted at Bloodgrue, and then at his deposit slip. "This is legitimate alright. Here are your two Flairs. I never heard of anyone doing the trip one way on foot in less than three days. My gods … I will hire you when I need someone. Well done dragoman. You made me a believer."

He pushes two gold Flairs over to Bloodgrue, as Bloodgrue take another bite of roasted quail.

Annelee appears lost in the extravagant meal before her, and the company she is in. Awed at the ease Bloodgrue sits with them, even though to her, he appears to be little more than barely older than a child and to be of lower-middle class.

The evening continues with small talk. Then Bloodgrue sleeps in the living room on the couch. Annelee has the solitude of a small bedroom to herself, courtesy of Bloodgrue's coin purse and Ottar's house.

We continue on …

In the next episode seventeen, 'Lilla'

While in Teptun Square and Market Bloodgrue is looking for work. Finding work with Potter Lilla he also finds an admirer with more than a little appreciation for Bloodgrue.

Awesome! You finished an episode of '*Bloodgrue*'.

Let us know what you think of it by going to this this link: www.inupress.ca While you are there, you should join the Inevitable Unicorn Press e-mail subscription list to receive news and updates about work from our authors such as; Rusty Knight, Brian Hill and Aria. When you sign up for the e-mail list, you will receive a free pdf. This free pdf changes with time. In February 2016 the gift was a copy of Rusty Knight's biography of the protagonists, the Black Swans, from his novel, '*Laret*'. Later in 2016, the bonus is an issue from the serial series, '*Lanis*'.

While on the home page of InUPress.ca leave a comment telling us what you think of our author's work, or the website. We appreciate your time and we will respond to questions and comments.

Thank you for reading.
Yours,
Rusty Knight of Inevitable Unicorn Press.
www.inupress.ca

As producer at InUPress.ca and author of the Bloodgrue serial short-story series, I thank you for reading Bloodgrue.

Rusty Knight

To be continued with Bloodgrue Volume 4: Attractions
Which will be found at InUPress.ca and Amazon

Previous books in the series available at www.inupress.ca and Amazon:
- *Bloodgrue Volume 1: Fare Where!*
- *Bloodgrue Volume 2: Breaths*